A Sports I CAN READ Book

On Your Mark, Get Set, Go!

The First All-Animal Olympics

by Leonard Kessler

D0045202

HARPER & ROW, PUBLISHERS
New York, Evanston, San Francisco, London

ON YOUR MARK, GET SET, GO!
Copyright © 1972 by Leonard Kessler

Trade Standard Book Number: 06-023152-1
Harpercrest Standard Book Number: 06-023153-X
Library of Congress Catalog Card Number: 72-76516

*To my favorite
runners, jumpers,
hurdlers, Olympic stars,
and friends of field and track.*

Chi Cheng   Ursula Nordstrom
Bob Seagren   Neil Amdur
Kip Keino   Red Smith
Babe Didrikson   Ed Coffey
Jesse Owens   Howard Cosell
Ralph Boston   Dr. Delano Meriwether
Jim Ryun   Coach Joe Healy
Arlene Klinkscale   Roy Fishman
Lili Kessler   Paul Roberts

The Newspaper

Rabbit found the newspaper
in the woods.

"What does it say?" he asked.

"I don't know. I can't read,"
said Dog.

"I can't read it," said Frog.

"Who can read?" asked Rabbit.

5

"Not me," said Worm.

"Not me," said Duck.

"Hey, here comes Owl," said Cat.

6

"Owl, can you read?" he asked.

"Not me. I never went
to school," said Owl.

"Well, who *can* read?" asked Frog.

"I can read some words,"
said Turtle.

He put on his glasses.

"It says SPORTS."

"Hey! Sports!" said Dog.

"Baseball," said Cat.

"Touchdown!" yelled Frog.

"Let's play," said Rabbit.

"No, no—not those games.
It says OLYMPIC GAMES,"
said Turtle.

"What are Olympic Games?"
asked Worm.

The New York Times

SPORTS

OLYMPIC GAMES

SCORE

U.S.A.	120
FRANCE	97
ITALY	119
ENGLAND	117
CHINA	1041

STANDING BROAD JUMP

POLE VAULT

By NEIL AMDUR

THE OLYMPIC GAMES TODAY FEATURED SOME OUTSTANDING PERFORMANCES BY WORLD FAMOUS ATHLETES SUCH AS ROY FISHMAN, JAMES "JIM" AHTES, DOT HELLER, B.J. McCABE, MURRAY BRIZELL, BOB HAGEN, JOHN ROST, DAN DANIELS, PAUL ROBERTS, AND AUDREY KAUFMANN.

THE GREAT JUMPERS WERE PAUL KESSLER, BRENT SLOBODY, FREDA OLMSTEAD, KIM KESSLER, STEVE GERSON, HERB SILVERMAN, LAURIE KARP, AND BEV PERNA.

THE SHOT PUT WINNER WAS SYD ROBBINS OF MIAMI.

400 METER RACE WAS WON BY PHIL RUBEN FROM SPOKANE, WASHINGTON.

DAVE BOLTON SET A NEW WORLD'S RECORD TODAY WITH A JUMP OF 19 FEET. RUTH TRISTRAM WON THE HIGH JUMP. FRANK GOECKEL PLACED SECOND IN THE 1500 METER RACE.

"Look at the pictures,"

said Owl.

"See?" said Turtle.

"There are lots of races.

10

OLYMPIC GAMES

GREAT SPRINTERS WERE BOBBY HOPP, JERI HELLER, JANICE FRIED, CAROL BECK, JUDY BUSTER, ETHEL KESSLER, MOE GLICK, PEARL REISS, PETE KIRSCHENBAUM, NORA SILVERMAN AND ELLIE LEWIS.

THOSE WHO DID WELL IN THE MILE RACE WERE FRAN MANUSHKIN, BARBARA BORACK, BARBARA DICKS, LILI KESSLER, DOROTHY ANGER, MAUREEN O'DAY, JANET POTTER, GENE ZION, RUDY MARINACCI, BARRY WILSON, CARL KRAFT, HUGH STURDY, MAL WEBER, WAYNE STEARNS, JEANETTE CAINES, JOYCE HOPKINS, LINC HAYNES,

SHEILA LEVINE, ROZ NOBLE, ARLENE KLINKSCALE, ALAN SUGARMAN, WILLIAM PEARLSTIEN, DANIELLE NORFLEET, JUDY BUNYAR, STEVE ADLER, LYNN PERNA, AND LARRY ISAACS.

THE RELAY RACE WAS WON BY URSULA NORDSTROM, NANCY JEWELL, ELLEN RUDIN AND NINA. THE HIGH HURDLE RACE WAS WON BY CHARLOTTE ZOLOTOW. THE 100 METER DASH WAS WON BY SUE HIRSCHMANN, AVA WEISS WAS SECOND.

THE HIGH JUMP WINNER WAS TOMMY BARATTA, IRV BARRON SECOND, SCOTTY BOUCHARD THIRD.

THE CROWD WAS OVER FIFTY THOUSAND. THE WEATHER WAS PERFECT. THE TEAM DOCTORS WERE DR. A.H. LEVERE, DR. DAVID BERNSTIEN, DR. GERRY RUTHEN, DR. SIDNEY BERIZEN, DR. SERGE BLUMENFELD, AND DR. S. BERSON, NEW CITY. DR. AL BERMAN, D.D.S CHECKED THE ATHLETES' TEETH.

There are hopping races,

there are jumping races,

and there are running races.

That's what Olympic Games are."

11

"Wow! That looks like fun,"

said Frog.

"Let's have our own Olympics,"

said Rabbit.

"I will win every race,"

Duck said.

"Oh, you ducks can't run.

You waddle," giggled Frog.

"Well, I waddle fast," said Duck.

She waddled off.

"Come back, Duck," said Frog.

"I was only joking."

Picking the Teams

"Let's pick teams," said Frog.

"We are a team,"

said Duck to Dog.

"We are the Yankees."

14

"Frog and me," said Rabbit.

"We are the Tigers."

"And we are the Pirates,"

said Turtle and Cat.

"Good," said Owl.

"That makes three teams.

And *I* will be the coach."

"But what about me?" asked Worm.

"And what about us?"

asked three little birds.

"Oh yes," said Owl,

"everyone can do something

in the Olympics.

One of you birds can be the starter.

And the other two can be judges."

"Yippee!" chirped the birds.

16

Teams

Yankees	Dog and Duck
Tigers	Frog and Rabbit
Pirates	Turtle and Cat

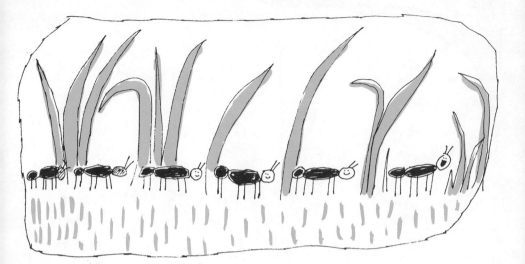

"We can be the starting line,"

said the ants.

"And I will make the finish line,"

said Spider.

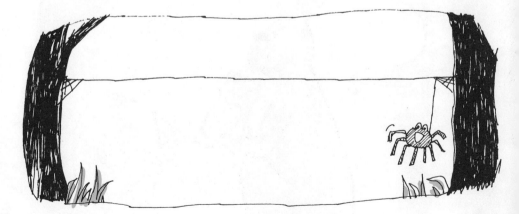

"Hey guys, what about me?"

asked Worm.

"Now each of you

has something to do,"

said Owl.

"Hey, how about me?"

yelled Worm.

"You? What can you do?"

asked Duck.

"You can't run.

You can't hop.

You can't jump.

You can't do anything!"

"I can. I can do something.

I can wiggle!" said Worm.

"Well, there are no

wiggling races," said Dog.

"You can be

the cheerleader," said Owl.

"The cheerleader?" said Worm.

"Yes," said Owl.

"And if anyone drops out,

then you can be on a team.

Okay?" asked Owl.

"Okay," said Worm.

"I will be the cheerleader."

Getting in Shape

"First, we must get in good shape," said Owl.

"What is that?" asked Frog.

"We must eat good food," said Owl.

"That's great," said Frog.

"I am hungry now!"

"No, no!" yelled Owl.

"No eating now or before a race.

It will slow you down.

First, we must exercise.

We must run, jump, and hop."

"And waddle," said Duck.

"And wiggle!" said Worm.

"We must do push-ups,"

said Owl.

"Okay everybody,

let's do push-ups.

1-2-3-4, 1-2-3-4.

Come on, Rabbit, work harder.

Good girl, Worm.

That's the way to do it.

Come on, Duck.

You can do better,"

Owl shouted.

"That Owl is a big boss,"
said Duck.

"She is not doing push-ups."

"Coaches don't run races,"
said Owl.

All that week they did push-ups.

They ran,

they hopped,

they skipped,

they jumped.

They wiggled and waddled.

They were in good shape now.

29

"The big Olympics
start tomorrow,"
said Owl. "Let's all get
a good night's sleep."
That night
Cat, Rabbit, Frog, and Worm
went to bed very early.
Duck and Turtle
went to bed at nine o'clock.
But what about Dog?
Dog did not go to sleep
until very, very late.

The next morning

everybody was ready

for the big Olympic parade.

Everybody but Dog.

"Boy, am I sleepy," he said.

Owl led the parade.

Then came the teams.

Next marched

the three little birds,

the ant family, and Spider.

Dog was next to last

because he was so tired.

And at the very end of the parade

little Worm wiggled.

The First Race

"The first race will be

running and jumping," said Owl.

"The first one

who jumps over all the hurdles

wins the race."

Dog, Rabbit, and Turtle

went to the starting line.

"If I am the starter,"

asked little Bird,

"do I go *Tweet tweet?*"

"Oh no," said Owl.

"Then how will I start

the races?" asked little Bird.

35

"You will say

On your mark, get set, go!

Got it?" asked Owl.

"Got it," said little Bird.

"And remember,"
said Owl to the racers,
"no stepping over
the starting line."
"And no stepping *on*
the starting line,"
said the ants.

"Okay," said little Bird.

"On your mark, get set, go!"

Off went Rabbit over the hurdles.

Off went Dog over the hurdles.

Off went Turtle to the first hurdle.

"I can't jump so well," said Turtle.

So Turtle went *under* the hurdles.

Rabbit crossed the finish line first.

Dog was second

because he was so tired.

And Turtle was last.

He was very, very sad.

"Let's have two prizes," said Owl.

"One for Rabbit,

who went *over* all of the hurdles.

And one for Turtle,

who went *under* all of the hurdles."

Worm led the cheer.

"Rabbit, Rabbit

Bim, Boom, Bah!

Turtle, Turtle

Rah! Rah! Rah!"

"I won a prize," said Turtle.

He smiled.

Worm wiggled over to Owl.

"I am ready to be on a team, Coach.

Any time you need me."

"Not now. Not yet," said Owl.

"But keep in shape till I call you."

The Hopping Race

"The next big race will be

the hopping race," Owl said.

"Hopping!" yelled Frog.

"Now that is my race."

He was munching his lunch.

"Owl told us not to eat

before a race," said Rabbit.

"It slows you down."

"Who cares what that old Owl says.
I am the fastest hopper here,
and I am hungry," said Frog.
He gobbled more food.
Soon he was stuffed.

"Line up for the hopping race,"

Owl said.

"Hey, Coach," said Worm.

"Put me in this race. I am ready."

"Not this race," said Owl.

"But keep in good shape."

"Okay, Coach," said Worm,

"I will do more push-ups!"

Duck, Cat, and Frog

went to the starting line.

"On your mark, get set, go!"

shouted little Bird.

Off hopped Cat. Hop. Hop.

Off hopped Duck. Hop. Hop.

Frog tried to hop too.

"Hop, Frog, Hop!" yelled Rabbit.

"I can't hop," said Frog.

"I am too full."

Cat hopped over the finish line first.

Duck was second.

And fat Frog just sat there. Plop.

He never left the starting line.

"How about a cheer for Cat?"

said Owl.

"Okay, Coach," said Worm.

"Pitter pitter pat,

pitter pitter pat.

Yay! Yay!

Cat, Cat, Cat."

Worm sat down.

"I could win a race too,"

said Worm,

"if they only gave me a chance."

The Big Team Relay Race

"All teams line up

for the big team relay race,"

Owl said.

Dog, Frog, and Turtle

went to the starting line.

Duck, Rabbit, and Cat

waited down the track.

Frog and Turtle

each had a little stick.

"Where is my stick?" asked Dog.

"Who has the stick?" asked Owl.

"Get a stick. I need a stick!"

yelled Dog.

Worm wiggled over to Owl.

"I am ready, Coach," said Worm.

"Hey, Worm," said Owl.

"You can be Dog's stick!"

"Wow! I am on a team!"

said Worm. "I'm a Yankee!"

"Okay," said Owl. "Each of you

must run with your stick.

Then pass it on

to your other team member.

And remember," said Owl,

"the stick must cross

the finish line."

"Okay," said little Bird.

"On your mark, get set, go!"

Zoom! Down the track they ran.

Cat, Rabbit, and Duck were waiting.

"Here they come," yelled Duck.

Turtle gave his stick to Cat.

Frog gave his stick to Rabbit.

And Dog gave his stick to Duck.

Zoom! Cat, Rabbit, and Duck

ran down the track.

"Duck is winning,

Duck is winning!" yelled Dog.

Duck smiled and waved

to the cheering crowd.

She tripped over her big web feet

and fell into a big mud puddle.

Squoosh!

"Get up, Duck," shouted Dog.

"Yikes," yelled Duck,

"I am stuck in the mud!"

"Don't worry, Duck," said Worm.

"I will win the race for our team."

Worm wiggled and wiggled.

She wiggled past the finish line—

first!

"Worm is the winner!" yelled Spider.

"The Yankees win!" shouted Dog.

"Let's give a cheer

for Worm," yelled Owl.

"Squiggle squiggle,

Who can wiggle?

Wiggle wiggle

Wiggle Worm.

Yay, yay, Worm!"

"That is the first time

I ever saw a stick win a race,"

said Frog.

"I am not a stick.

I am a Yankee!" yelled Worm.

They all laughed.

The Olympics End

It was the greatest Olympics

ever held in the woods.

Everyone ran and hopped,

and skipped and jumped,

and waddled and wiggled,

and laughed and giggled.

61

Owl made a speech:

"Everybody *did* something,

and everybody *learned* something."

"I learned to get to bed early

before a race," said Dog.

"I learned not to eat

before a race," said Frog.

"I learned to keep on running

and not wave," said Duck.

"I learned that

if you keep in good shape,

you can win a race," said Worm,

"even if all you can do

is wiggle."

"Wow! Olympics are fun," said Dog.

"Let's do this again

next year," said Spider.

"Three cheers for Owl,"

said the three little birds.

"Rah! Rah! Rah!"

"**Now** can I have something

to eat?" asked Frog.